Soft Domination

Alpha, Monster, Euthanasia, Interracial, Cuckold, Sensual erotica for man and woman erotica romance & erotica fantasies for couples or singles

Lana Kendra

it wasn't bought for your personal use only, go back to your favorite ebook retailer and buy your copy. Thank you for acknowledging this author's efforts.

Table of Contents

Content Warning

Due to its sexual content, this book is only for those over the age of legal adulthood. There are some topics with a lot of foul language. All of the characters are at least eighteen years old.

Introduction

Are you in search of an exciting and thrilling book to read? Look no further than this extensive collection of Erotic Suspense book. I offer a wide range of genres, including Romantic Erotica, Fantasy, and Urban BDSM Fiction, to cater to even the most discerning reader. Whether you enjoy Anthologies, Westerns, or Paranormal Romance, I have something to suit your taste. My collection also includes Poetic Folklore, Interracial, Black & African American Literary Criticism, and Gothic Horror for those who crave a deeper and darker reading experience. If you're interested in Futuristic, LGBTQ+, Short Stories, or Lesbian literature, my diverse range of options will keep you captivated. Additionally, I offer Humorous, Victorian, New Adult, and College Women's Psychological Mysteries for those seeking a lighter but equally engaging read. Furthermore, My Fairy Tale Collections,

Transgender, Contemporary Western, Bisexual, and Poetry genres will transport you to different worlds and explore a variety of themes. For my Teen and Young Adult readers, I have a selection of European Geography, Cultures, eBooks, Loners, Outcasts, Mythology, Folk Tales, and much more. With such a wide array of options to choose from, you'll never run out of thrilling and enchanting stories to immerse yourself in.

It is important to emphasize that this content is exclusively intended for individuals who are 18 years of age or older.

Soft Domination

Where do I begin? The decision to proceed in a different direction probably occurred a few months ago, right before college graduation. Perhaps I wouldn't be writing this now if I had come from a regular family—a nice, straightforward family with less ostentation of money and more common sense—because then, perhaps, what occurred would never have happened. Do I have to regret that? Really, I'm not sure. In any case, I was just starting to settle into what I thought would be my forever life at that point. It was the life I had grown up expecting, and the life my friends and parents expected of me. Thanks to my family's connections, I was able to get an internship editing legal briefs at a reputable Manhattan law company. My main goal was to use the time between graduation and my anticipated marriage. I had started talking to my fiancé about our future plans. Everything seemed so planned, so bright. Our parents were enthusiastically organizing a lavish wedding.

A couple of us at a famous upstate institution that used to be exclusively for women decided to rebel against the strict Protestant indoctrination that had been our usual upbringing as we approached the end of our senior year. Yes, a lot of kids do that, but maybe you have to go farther to establish your independence the higher you are on the false social ladder. Well, that's the appearance. Of course, when we made the decision to go into the city and investigate the less glamorous side of the Village, I didn't really realize it would be that risky. It's just a small bit of revolt.

It's how I got to know Sly. Oh, I realized he wasn't a royal. He seemed disheveled and shady, but hey, I had something to prove. He expressed his desire to take us around the Village and procure some quality cannabis. Our group's lone seemingly rational member, Amanda, objected.

"You guys are nuts! What do you know about this guy? Who knows what he could get us into."

"Oh, Christ," Sly exclaimed. "What a bunch of princesses! You're so used to your privileges you don't dare take a chance. If I showed up in a limo, you'd jump to go with me, wouldn't you. But no, I don't look all-college, so why trust me. Go fuck yourselves then."

We couldn't refuse the challenge, though. We'd prove to him that we weren't just a bunch of snarky society girls. I was afraid, but I wasn't sure how the other girls felt. However, I reasoned that if you're going to go adventuring, you really had to go adventuring. And feeling afraid is only one aspect of it. Whoa, what an idiot!

"Oh please," I said. That's me, the leader, saying, "Don't be a bunch of pussies. I'm here to have some fun. Are you with me or not!" Gosh! However, I suppose I persuaded enough.

After sharing her thoughts with us about our "adventure," Amanda departed to return to her studies. After Sly phoned some of his friends, we went out to bars together until we were all pretty well greased. I suppose I could use that as an explanation, but I believe the actual reason Sly and his friends took us all to that run-down motel was that by that point, we had kind of committed to each other. Yes, we did screw up. It wasn't terrific, either. While some guy was slobbering into my pussy, I believe I passed out. In any case, by dawn we were abandoned and alone, our credit cards and valuables gone, and our pockets emptied.

Putting aside our pride, we called Amanda to come fetch us, promising to keep the incident a secret and to just accept our losses without talking about it. We cancelled all the credit cards after visiting health services to get checked out for sexually transmitted diseases just to be careful. It appeared to be over after that, at least for a few weeks, until I started missing my period. Aw sh*t! After taking the test, I was knocked out pretty good. Apparently, one of those bastards had fucked me bareback. What a waste of birth control tablets!

It was obvious that I had to give up the baby before I started showing. Sadly, I knew of no one I could trust who was also an abortionist who refused to answer questions. The only place to go was that one. I forced myself to swallow my pride and my rage and found Sly.

"Not my problem," he informedly remarked. "I never laid a hand on you."

I answered, "That's not the point." "I'm willing to pay. I just need it done quietly, and soon."

He consented to tell me how he would respond. The

following day, he texted me his phone number. That was my call. I won't rehash the specifics here, but the task was completed.

I could move on from that and get on with my life, I reasoned.

Naturally, things did not work out that way.

I received a text from Sly a month or so after graduation, right when I was starting to settle into my new job and apartment in the city. The text included some really amazing pictures of me lying there on the bed, naked, with my legs spread wide, this Black guy's head deep in my crotch, and at least multiple people's sperm decorating my chin and breasts. As if that weren't enough, a copy of the abortionist's bill was also provided in the text!

Sly's message was simple: "Give me a call when you get a chance. I could use some help in picking out the best pics to send to mom and dad. If you need help paying this bill, your kid's dad will help, though he's pretty pissed that you didn't let him know, and he's threatening to take you to court over it."

It was obvious that I was hooked—and good. My entire existence fell apart in the span of one fucking night. Though I like to think I've moved over the prejudices I was raised with in our lily-white Connecticut town, I was aware that my parents and other people who mattered to me would not be pleased with that small scene of racial peace. It was all up to me. Call me Sly.

We made plans to meet in the city at his apartment. A few rooms in a middling apartment building on the west side, a bed and dresser in the bedroom, a couch and a few chairs in the living room, and a tiny kitchenette that appeared to have never been used—not a horrible place. There were two closed windows. He took a seat beside me on the couch and explained the terminology to me. He informed me of the cost of the images and related content. It was evident that I could not raise the necessary funds without causing a great deal of controversy.

"Well then, honey, I guess you're just going to have to work it off. For starters, I could use a good blow job." (Sly was dressed to impress!) "Take off that blouse and let's see what you got." .

It wasn't as though I had never heard of blow jobs, either. For crying out loud, I'm not a virgin. Yes, I had previously performed manual labor, but only for individuals I liked and could gratify in that way. But I'd never taken an interest in the oral stuff. It appeared really dirty and embarrassing, to be honest. But at this point, I was unable to envision a way out. Everything for the first time. So, under Sly's careful observation, I undid my blouse and removed it like a nice girl. After thanking me with a whistle, he urged me to remain motionless and continued to walk around me. He removed my bra.

He remarked, "Jesus, you got a real rack, Babe," and then he helped himself to my breasts, licking and pinching my nipples till they hardened like little traitors. I must have looked blank when they said, "Ok, assume the position." I did as he said, "Down on your knees, dummy. Now." How else could I help?

In order to get a clean view of my face, he first took my hair, which was worn long back then, and brushed it back. After that, he played around with my mouth a little by parting my lips, wetting them with his fingers, and lubricating them with my saliva. He slowly backed away and dropped his pants, as like he was trying to give me a show—which I most definitely didn't need. It's impossible for a female to make it through high school, let alone college, without encountering some guys, particularly if she's attractive and has an amazing physique (yeah, like me. Deal with it). But this one, my goodness! I had no idea how in the world I was going to get that thing in my mouth. I think I appeared surprised.

Sly grinned and replied, "Nice one, hunh. Gonna stretch that tight little upscale mouth of yours a bit, but trust me, once you get it in there you're gonna love it."

He gave his dick a few strokes to get some pre-cum. He dripped some over his fingers, then dabbed it onto my lips and pressed his finger to my mouth to sample it. He then pushed in on me, pressing his steaming dick on my lips to further moisten them with his pre-cum. It was very terrible. He pushed his hips into me and gripped my head so I couldn't pull away, and I just knelt there frightened to move. The next thing I knew, his enormous cockhead was fiercely pressing against my teeth and had forced my lips apart.

With a "C'mon, girl," he spoke. "Open up. Relax, you're gonna like it. Trust me." Yes. Yes. But in order to regain my freedom, I had no choice but to finish it. In addition, how awful could it possibly be? Several of my friends had tried it, and a few of them even said they enjoyed it. And to be honest, I was a little interested. I opened up as I was instructed to do.

Sly didn't take long. My lips quivered as that massive head pushed through them, propelled by its own pre-cum. Once they entered the smaller shaft, they began to loosen up a little. The nasty thing was in my mouth for almost three inches before I even noticed it. Jesus, that was so simple to put on my lips! It felt heavy, as if it belonged on my bottom lip, and I could feel it moving along my tongue. I wasn't expecting it to be that terrible, though. It was so vibrant and lively, it was pulsating. I could sense the firm, substantial core of it beneath the surface of its smooth, silky exterior. Very unique, in fact. He continued to probe into my mouth, and I could feel every small bump and irregularity on the shaft. Thankfully, he finally stopped before reaching my throat, and I was able to adjust to having his cock in my mouth.

With a "good girl," he said. "You're doin' fine, so far. It feels real good in there, don't it? Nice and fat and warm. And full, too. Now, you just relax, and I'm gonna make your day."

He then begins to slide in and out of my mouth without ever removing the head of his cock. My mouth begins to moisten very quickly, which facilitates his cock slide and increases my level of comfort. Despite everything, I relaxed a little and started to investigate the novel feelings I was experiencing because I was starting to get used to this. I was immediately struck by the fact that it was genuinely seductive! I knew I was becoming damp down there because I could feel my breasts getting firmer and my clit tingling irrefutably. I really wanted to reach down and give myself a self-rub, but I decided to merely move my thighs slightly in the hopes that Sly wouldn't notice.

Sly continued to stroke in and out, at times moving more quickly than others and at other times pausing for a brief period of time. He was breathing faster and harder, and I could feel the tension rising in them when he placed both of his hands on my head to calm it. I too was becoming agitated by his arousal! I began sucking on him, a little hesitant at first, then more enthusiastic. It was as though we were building on each other. He was breathing very quickly, and I knew he was going to cum in my mouth at any moment. I was a little afraid again at that point as I had no idea how much cum he had for me, what it would taste like, or if I would choke on it or be able to manage it. Was it something I was meant to swallow, or could I spit it out without upsetting him? But by then, he didn't give a damn about anything except his impending climax.

At that moment, he firmly grasped my head and pressed his penis far within me, holding it there. I felt the large vein on the underside of his cock bulge, and I heard him gasp and groan. He seemed to be preparing to inject me with sperm, which caused my cock to swell and get heavy. Then he arrived! His cock's tip shot semen, which struck the roof of my mouth with a strong feel. It felt really warm! However, it was quickly followed by more, and his salty-sweet discharge filled my lips in a matter of seconds. There was so much of it, God! I was afraid of choking when I tried to swallow with his enormous cock in my mouth. His sperm collected on and under my tongue as my cheeks blew up. A few started to seep past my lips and embrace the aching prick. The warm discharge splashed onto my breasts and ran down my chin. Nevertheless, he continued to cum. If I wasn't already engrossed in the fury by that point, damn you. I was so riled up by all of his panting and moaning and the huge cock throbbing and squirting his semen into me that I almost came myself! To set me off, all I would have needed was a touch on my clit. This wasn't awful at all, hell!

To be honest, I was a little let down when his ejaculations finally ceased, the last one coming out almost carelessly and dripping across my tongue. My mind was whirling with all these novel experiences by that point. A strange sense of pride that I had taken that large, fat cock in my mouth, brought it to a crazy peak, and taken his copious discharge was mixed in. I really must be a lady.

After he stopped cumming, Sly rested his hands on my head to prevent me from pulling away, and he remained his cock in my mouth for a considerable amount of time. To be honest, I didn't mind because I wasn't in a rush at the time. I was still processing my feelings. Eventually, though, he gave way, and the large object came out of my mouth and started to gradually lose its air even as I was watching. It leaked some sperm I had forgotten to remove, but I was still able to save a decent mouthful. The majority of it went down in one large gulp, and I felt the warm bulk go down my throat and effortlessly fall in my stomach. I could feel his taste chilling on my breasts and chin as it filled my mouth. I was surprised that I only felt a little warm inside instead of nauseous.

"Sweetie, for a princess you're not a bad cocksucker," Sly replied. It may surprise you to learn that when he stated that, I experienced a strange sense of pride. However, I was still rather perplexed by everything that had occurred in the previous few minutes. I collected the remnants of my self-respect that I could.

"Well," I replied. "I hope you're satisfied. Now let's have those pics and the other stuff and I'm outa here."

It didn't seem like it would be that simple. It also wasn't.

With a kind of amused skepticism, Sly gazed at me.

"Jesus, Princess, you have one hell of a high opinion of yourself, don't you. You were good, but just how much do you think one blow job is worth? I mean, I could get sucked off by a professional for maybe hundred bucks, and you're just an amateur with a lot to learn. A good one I admit, but still an amateur. Maybe fifty bucks or so? You owe me a hell of a lot more than fifty bucks. So, darlin', if you're gonna work it off with your mouth you got a lot more suckin' to do, don't ya think?"

By now, I was furious. "You're a real bastard, you know that? I did what you asked, and now I want my stuff. I'm not gonna spend my life sucking you off, you son of a bitch."

Sly grinned and raised his hands in a conciliatory gesture. With a "now, now, honey," he spoke. "Much as I enjoyed that (and I know you did too), there's a limit as to how many times I want it. Not, I'm afraid, enough times for you to work off what you owe me. However, I'm sure we can work something out. I've got some friends who would just love to meet you. And hell, maybe you could even do some free-lance work to earn some extra. Plenty of guys patrol the streets and bars around here lookin' for someone like you. You'd be surprised how fast you could work it off if you're willin' to work hard at it."

And it was the beginning of it all.

A week later, Sly invited me back to his apartment after work. I had been dreading this for the entire week, but I decided to take the necessary action because I truly couldn't see any other way out of it without his permanently wrecking my life. I dressed as subduedly as possible, hopped in a cab, and pressed the doorbell. He opened the door for me, examining every inch of me and grinning to let me know he understood why I looked the way I did.

He said, "I'm glad you showed up, luv." He handed me a package that felt way too light and said, "You really are as smart as you look. I think we're gonna make this work out just fine. But first, get out of those clothes and put this on." My spirit fell. "Go on, go into the bedroom there and put it on."

As they say, "In for a penny, in for a pound." I was raised with the belief that once you set your mind to a task, no matter how repulsive it may be, you should just finish it. But when I opened the parcel I nearly fainted. The small amount of material within was almost translucent, silky black nylon. The top of the panties was tied with a simple bow at the front, and the crotch was split. Absent a bra. Fuck! Like a wet fantasy straight out of Victoria's Secret. It was beyond me why guys required all of this gear in order to get off. Well, I thought, whatever it takes to get through this.

Sly's eyes widened immediately as I emerged from the bedroom, and I felt more nude than if I had nothing on at all. But if I showed him, I'd be condemned. I returned the smile, nonchalantly strolled over to the couch, sat down, and crossed my legs as best I could.

"Jesus Christ, you look good in that," Sly remarked with appreciation.

"Yeah, well thanks, I guess. But if you don't want me to spoil it by breaking out in goose bumps and turning blue, you'd better turn up the heat in this place. This isn't the warmest outfit I've ever worn. And by the way, you got anything to drink around here?" I was so cool.

"Yes, Babe," he replied. Like I didn't know that vodka wouldn't leave a trace on my breath. "I don't want you getting looped before we even get started, but maybe a good shot of Vodka'll set you up." He did, however, pour me a stiff one.

I thought he would get right to it, but instead we just there awkwardly silently for ten or so minutes. After giving his watch a few quick glances, the doorbell rang. He stood up and made his way toward the door, but paused, spun around, and gave me a close-up look. He reached over to adjust my hair slightly and gave my cheeks a quick push to make them a little redder. He strolled over and unlocked the door after giving his work one more look. This attractive, well-dressed Black man entered. After shaking hands, Sly asked, "So, what do you think? We even?" while pointing me out to the man.

The guy gave me a hard look, like if I were a brand-new automobile or something. Guess I made it through inspection. "Maybe," he responded. "If she's as good as you say she is."

At that point, Sly brought the man over to sit on the couch. He answered, "All right, let her see it."

At that point, the black man takes off his pants and cock. I had never before seen a Black man's cock. In spite of not being stiff, it appeared really large.

He uttered, "I dunno." "She looks scared. You sure she's good?"

"Believe in me," Sly added. "All right, you're on. Reach up and touch it," he then stated to me.

I squeezed back into the couch, reached out as far away from me as I could, and hesitantly touched the guy's cock because, well, I was a bit terrified, a little in awe, and a lot shy. It was cozy and velvety. It had a rather innocent appearance, and the mahogany hue was rather appealing. I gave it a slight raise and examined it, swiveling it about as if I were a cock inspector. What an idiot. However, hesitant or not, my touch felt right, and that cock began to rise up, grow thick, and harden. Touch of magic, I suppose.

That's when Sly grabbed my head and dragged me forward until that expanding cock was all I could see.

"Smile, please," he urged. I attempted to move away, but he restrained me by holding my head. He pushed my head forward until my lips contacted the man's prick with one hand under my chin and the other behind my head. To the touch, it wasn't at all unpleasant. It was quite pleasant and cozy. His pre-cum tasted salty to me. I tentatively kissed it.

Sly grinned and replied, "She's ok, just give her a minute. She'll be fine. You're her first Black guy," in response to the guy giving her the fish-eye.

With a scowl, he nudged my head until the man's penis curled up about an inch into my mouth. It felt fairly normal and glided in with relative ease. In a way, it's warm. I let myself relax a little because it was still fairly soft and appeared to be harmless. Whether it was black or not, it was still just a manhood. It soon began to stiffen, growing into my mouth as it did so and becoming heavier, harder, and fatter in the process. That felt really different! It was growing longer and bigger, and I was starting to get a little anxious again. Eventually, though, it stopped, and even though it was very large, I felt like I could manage it. To be honest, I didn't feel too uncomfortable in there. Its gentle pulsation and warmth on my tongue were kind of nice. Regardless, he simply left it there for a minute, which allowed me the space I needed to come to terms with and adjust to it.

The Black guy pushed his cock further into me, presumably satisfied that I was no longer resisting him. Then he leaned down, untied my blouse's tie, and started petting my breast. This wasn't so bad, after all! He stroked and squeezed my breast in a very nice way that felt great. I leaned in to put my head closer to his groin and sat up taller to make myself more approachable. In order to give him more freedom, I reached around his cock, undid his belt, and let his pants drop open. He obviously thought the idea was cool, since he briefly removed his cock from my lips and removed his shorts and pants to provide me full access to all of his manly parts. He was naked after taking off his shirt. And he was pretty damn nice looking. Despite my nerves, I had to admit that I was impressed. He then placed his hand on my head and resumed putting his penis in my mouth. Oh my, that went in so smoothly!

This man was so slick, my goodness! He was well aware of what he wanted from me and how to obtain it. He moved my body to get me exactly where he wanted me, largely with nudges and forceful hands rather than words. For the most part, I was barely aware of it. I simply followed his path, obediently. He had complete faith in his ability to control. He was not in a hurry, and neither was I. Though I like to think of myself as an independent woman, I discovered then that giving your body and will to someone who obviously understands what he's doing can be very damn sexy.

He pressed my shoulders back, bending forward in the process. I sat back, as he had instructed. Before long, my head was leaned back into the pillows and my back was resting against the back of the couch. The black man braced his hands on either side of my head as he got up on the couch and stepped over me. He replaced his prick in my mouth with a casual demeanor. I was a little uneasy at first because I thought I would have nowhere to go if he really jammed his prick into me, but he seemed content to just slowly stroke in and out a few inches at a time. I relaxed a little and let him move in and out of my mouth, holding onto his cock with my lips and supporting it with my tongue, as I quickly started to feel confident in him. I felt so good as he began caressing my breast once more. I gently massaged the inside of his leg, up to where my palm brushed against his balls as they swung with his movements, as a way to encourage him.

Sly, meantime, had been occupied. He had gone down on his knees in front of me while I was distracted by the cock in my face. The sensation of my legs spreading apart made me realize that, and the next thing I knew, he was in there, kissing my pussy and inserting his tongue remarkably far up my vagina. Thank God for crotchless underwear. I was beginning to feel fairly comfortable about things between the tongue in my vagina, the hand on my breast, and the cock stroking in my mouth. It wasn't the end of the world if this was how I was going to fulfill my obligation. In any case, as long as my fiancé and my family never find out about it.

I lost all sense of the outside world for a good minute as

Sly's skillful tongue found its way to my sweet spot. I was enveloped in a warm glow and completely enamored with everyone and everything when it returned, especially that incredibly tasty cock that was filling my mouth with warmth and its yearning for me.

I was really getting into it by then, circling my tongue over the tip and pressing it into the Black guy's slit while I enthusiastically sucked on his huge cock. As his balls bounced back and forth, I even reached up and caressed them. It felt good. Dense. I was still unsure about Black cum and how much of it there might be, but I started to look forward to having him shoot in my mouth. His balls were quite full. Stories concerning Black guys are common, and I suppose stereotypes never really go away.

But he was far from finished with me. I'm not sure how it happened—I guess I hadn't been focusing on anything other the tongue in my pussy and the cock in my mouth—

but somehow we ended up with the Black guy standing over me while I sat on the floor with my head resting back on the cushions and my back against the couch. I guess I must have been of assistance, but if so, I was unaware of it. This guy was suave and knew exactly what he wanted, like I mentioned. I was merely a passenger. His penis slid back into my mouth with ease, and he gave me a few quick strokes, varying in depth and tempo. Sly—may his tiny heart be blessed—had followed my pussy all the way to the floor with his hand and was still fidgeting with my moist vagina. In addition to the cock in my mouth, it felt incredibly good. I continued to stroke my man's inner thigh. Every now and then I held his balls in my palm and gave them a light squeeze, just for fun. I could hear his labored breathing.

After a minute or two of this, the Black man lifts me up into a kneeling position in front of him, stretches down, and places his hands under my armpits. He never took his cock out of my mouth, but for some reason, he was able to make me follow his every move. However, I believe I was helpful this time. The whole gymnastic thing intrigued me, so I was happy to follow the guy's lead and speculate about our next destination and the resolution of the situation.

I was on my knees staring at his highly aroused (and by this point, fairly recognizable) instrument. Perhaps he preferred a more conventional stance, or perhaps he wasn't too delighted about having Sly share me with him. Sly did nothing but stand up, watch, and hold his cock in his hand. I believe he was just as interested in what would come next as I was.

Finding out didn't take long. With one hand, the Black guy steadied my head while he began to stroke himself with the other, only letting the tip of his penis into my mouth. His breath grew sharper, and I could hear it. When he started to orgasm, I prepared to swallow his cum by holding onto his hips for support. However, he withdrew just as I was getting ready and even anticipating his hot sperm exploding in my lips. He stroked himself, nice and gently at first, then quicker and faster, keeping his glistening wet dick an inch or two away from my mouth. I thought I knew exactly what he wanted. I deduced that he desired to observe his sperm piercing me. Although I would have preferred it otherwise, I had already given him authority, so I chose to wait with my mouth hanging open.

While I waited, I couldn't help but fantasize about putting Black sperm in my mouth and how much of it, if the stories girls told were true, this dude might be about to fire into me. I gave in and opened my mouth just enough to satisfy everyone without making it impossible for me to quickly shut it if things grew too intense for me.

I could sense his penis quivering in close proximity to my lips. I extended my tongue to touch it. That satisfied him.

I felt a hot droplet of sperm on my tongue as he moaned. One of the spurts landed on my chin, and another struck my upper lip. I realized that if I gave him a landing zone, or an on-ramp, as it were, his cum would wind up in my mouth rather than all over my face, and that would be beneficial for both of us. I stick out my tongue even more. He quickly realized that he was smooth. As he proceeded to pump his load straight into my mouth, he moved in and rested the heavy head of his cock on my tongue. As each bolus of sperm blasted into me, I could feel its pulse. His seed was piling up quickly, and it felt shockingly heavy and warm in my mouth. Pretty sexy, too, especially with sighs of delight and deep breathing. By the way, my little sample revealed that Black cum tastes quite much like cum from White guys, and Black cum is truly white. Not shocking at all, I suppose. In any case, I opened up a little broader as I started to feel at ease in the circumstance. Nevertheless, he got some on my lips, chin, face, and neck in addition to my neck. He really did have plenty to spare, haha. The protracted buildup may have had an impact, in my opinion. Now that I think about it, if he had cummed like this before, when he was so far in my mouth, I don't think I could have managed it all without exposing myself.

His gasps and groans told me that he was having a great time. I also became entangled in it. But ultimately, he did run out of jism. By then, my mouth was somewhat full. However, as soon as he calmed down and stopped spitting, I sensed a hand gripping my shoulders and was shifted to the side. As soon as I opened my eyes, I saw Sly approaching his climax and stroking his cock. I was expecting another shot of cum, so I just parted my lips because I didn't know what else to do. Instead, Sly leaned down and completely undid my already-thin top, revealing my nude breasts, before saturating them with his own sperm. Some of his hot ejaculate stuck to my erect nipples, while some ran down the valley between them. I felt it settle on them.

He suddenly changed gears as his climax was about to an end, skillfully placed his prick in my mouth, and then fired the remainder of his load into it. I hadn't had time to swallow much of the Black guy's load, so now I had two loads in my mouth at once. It felt quite weird. Anyway, I remained motionless until Sly was done. Impressed by the quantity of ejaculations from two guys, I swirled the viscous warm pile around for a little while with my tongue, tasting it. I parted quickly at the Black guy's command, allowing the boys to see the results of their labor. The smiles indicated that they were pleased with what they witnessed. I then ingested the most of their semen. It required multiple attempts to get it all down because it was quite a bunch. A few unintentionally overflowed across my chin. They seemed to be having a great time at the concert. Guys enjoy showing off how big their loads are to themselves.

For a moment, their cocks drooped and softened as they stood there, appearing content with themselves. When they were finally clothed, I was kneeling on the floor with their sperm all over my lips, chin, and breasts. They ignored me the entire time.

Sly asked the Black man, "Well?" "We good? She was worth it like I told you?"

Yes, the Black guy replied. "Yeah, we're even. She was okay. Hey, you gonna be at the game Friday?"

"Why, you think you can win again? Luck runs out ya know."

After we finished getting dressed, they both grinned at their newfound friendship, and I got up and sat like a lump on the couch, feeling their cool, dry semen on my body. This negligee would have to be washed by Sly before it was used once more. If I were to do it, I'd be condemned.

The Black guy went, and I showered and got dressed. I then went up against Sly. "So, how much was I worth to you?"

"Well, you were pretty good, honey. You just worked off a $500 poker debt for me. Good work. So that gets credited to your account. You keep this up and we'll be square in no time, and you can get back to your cozy little princess life. But until then, you just be sure to be here when I call you and do what you're told."

"Tell me that I was not the stakes in some God damned poker game!" I replied.

His eyes grew wide, then wrinkled in laughter. He extended his hands in my direction.

"No, babe. Don't go getting all uptight. I bet real money. You just covered it for me."

"Ok, then. But don't get any ideas for the future. Bad

enough I have to do this for money. You have to leave me some dignity."

Sly merely moaned. I had to accept that as confirmation. I thought I had established some ground rules, at least.

That brought an end to my first indentured slavery session. Looked like this bizarre double life of a respectable legal intern by day and a party girl by night, if Sly called with a client, was what I had to look forward to from now on until I wiped my slate clean.

Which, two days later, he did. The same thing happened: I went up at his apartment, he gave me another strong vodka shot to calm my butterflies, and we sat there in awkward silence—at least from me—until the doorbell rang. This time, it was an older, quite average-looking man, around fifty years old. I was wearing my (clean) negligee while seated on the couch. Again, Sly pointed me out to the guy without even mentioning my name. The new person, like the Black one, seemed to like what he saw, too, since he smiled and gave Sly a little wad of cash. After giving a warm smile in return, Sly responded, "Great. She's all yours. Enjoy yourself." He settled into a cozy chair and lit a cigarette.

"What's your name, honey?" the guy asks as he approaches the couch and takes a position in front of me. I instantly made up a name, "Vicki. Vicki with an i." Sly gave me a thumbs-up and rolled his eyes over his shoulder. Fortunately, he was sensible enough to say nothing.

"I'm going to fuck you now, Vicki with an i," he remarked in a casual manner. Nice to know. Just in case I mistook his request for a semi-naked girl he had just paid for for a discussion on Kierkegaardian existentialism. He undid the bow on my top with extreme care, stretched the nylon, and stood staring gratefully at my breasts like a child unwrapping a Christmas gift. He remarked, "You have very lovely breasts." Jesus, it sounded like he was about to do a gynecological exam. "You can leave the top on, it's quite sexy, but slip out of the panties, then lie down and let me get a good look at your pussy." Anyway, I followed instructions because he was paying.

As expected, he examines my treasure box closely while twitching my clit and widening his lips. It was weird, but in a good way. Evidently pleased with his discovery, he undressed (carefully folding his clothes) and positioned himself over me on the sofa. I saw the little drop of pre-cum that was gathering on the tip of his prick as it grew. "Well," he replies. "Now I'm going to fuck you, and you will either like it or I will expect you to do a very convincing imitation of liking it."

With that, he climbs over me and instantly thrusts his firm prick inside me. Well, that hurt a little because I wasn't lubricated. He started sawing in and out of me, so I just bit my lip and held on. Fortunately, I was able to lubricate rather quickly, which allowed the discomfort to immediately subside and allow me to enjoy myself. Though I didn't really need to pretend, I nevertheless hammered it out and began to breathe heavily and grunt. Strangely enough, I started to feel extremely excited about my own acting and soon I wasn't just acting; I was actually taking part. He continued to thrust deeper, so my hips began to move in time with his movements.

He was really getting into it now. He took hold of my breasts and massaged them. His hips rose and fell, his cock dug more and deeper into me, and his breaths were rapid and shallow. He wasn't going to last long at that rate, and a minute or two later, he forcefully pressed his groin on my pussy. His cock was almost pushing against my cervix, and suddenly he inserted himself into me. Oh my goodness, that warm pouring in me and his pulsating cock pinching my clit did the trick for me. I didn't even have to fake it.

He really did cum. My vagina filled up quickly, and I felt his sperm squeezing out of his cock and down between my legs. Even when I moaned and squirted, he persisted, clinging to my breasts for dear life and gasping with ecstasy.

Finally, he was empty. His breathing slowed as he fell to my chest, nestling his head between my moist breasts. With deliberate slowness, he withdrew from me. Then he performed a strange thing. He moved down my body until he was able to press his face into my vagina. I could feel and hear him suckling on our shared fluids, trying to lick them all up. Strange, but yet kind of cute, I have to admit.

He stood. Having been observing our performance the entire time, Sly gave him (not me, of course) a towel to wipe himself off, which he duly did. My most recent customer turned to face me as I lay there, my black negligee crumpled beneath my upper body, my hot thighs parted apart, his semen still staining my pussy hair.

He remarked, "You did very well." "Thank you."

Wasn't that courteous, then! However, I must admit that it gave me a positive self-image. Everyone enjoys being acknowledged for their hard work, isn't that right?

He dressed himself, thanked Sly as well (I watched with amusement as Sly had no idea how to react to that), and walked away.

I told Sly he was a nice person. "You can bring him again some time. And any more like him. So, how much did I make that time?"

Sly glanced at me. "Your little performance cost him $400. Take out my fee and you made $300 tonight."

"Your fee? What do you mean 'your fee'? Fuck, you just got a free show. Look at you. Your pants are wet from your own pre-cum! That's your 'fee'!"

"Hey, take it or leave it, babe. I bring them in. You fuck them. I get a commission. I gotta make a living, too. Ya want to go into business for yourself when I got nothin' for you, go right ahead, and good luck."

Alright, he had me.

"You know," I replied, "you're a right bastard."

Indeed, he replied. "I know. How's your ass?"

I regarded the sudden shift in subject twice. "What do you mean?"

"I mean, how's your ass. I got a client for you that wants it."

"You mean, he wants to fuck me in the ass? Forget it. I've never done that before and I'm sure not eager to try."

"Five hundred bucks says you ought to change your mind.

For this one I'll skip my commission. Consider it an investment for the future. Always good to have the help learn new skills."

"No way. Find someone else."

"Already set it up. He'll be here Thursday. If you're a no-show I'll have to add that $500 to your bill. Think about it."

I walked out. and returned to my apartment at home. and gave it some thought. ... appeared on Thursday.

It goes without saying that I was anxious. Sly ushered me in and settled me onto the sofa. "Vodka?" he questioned.

I said, "Make it a double."

He grinned. "Think that'll help? Sure, babe. You've got good instincts, anyway, even when you're a little oiled." Oh, a praise! Then what?

"Now, go get dressed. Oh, and I told this guy you were a virgin. There's an extra hundred in it for us. Keep that in mind." Like I had to be warned.

The doorbell took what felt like an eternity to ring. I leaped.

"Christ," said Sly. "You look like you're ready to run away. Sit the hell back, Cross your legs. Shoulders back. Lift those breasts. And for God's sake, relax. Don't look so uptight!"

"I thought I was supposed to be a virgin," I said. "How relaxed do you want me to be?"

Sly gave me a stern look for a few moment after that. There was definitely a hint of resentful respect in the glance.

The man, who was casually dressed in slacks and a shirt, was not ugly, Sly admitted. He was probably in his mid-thirties. He had on loafers.   Maybe a lawyer? Anyhow, something like a professional.

We completed the routine. Sly gestured for him to come look at me, and we exchanged money and palms. Next, Sly guided him to the sofa. The man examined me closely.

I can't remember what I responded when he asked, "What's your name, honey?" But he just replied, "Nice name. Nice body, too." Then he untied my top and asked me to get up and turn around once. I very demurely managed to take them down and step out of them without leaning over too much, intentionally trying to protect my ass. "Okay, let's have the panties off too." However, in vain.

"You have a very nice ass," he remarked with appreciation.

I did everything I could to "bend over a little." He gave me a really good, loving ass-kiss. I heard him undressing behind me.

Oh my, it was actually going to happen. "Okay, get down on your hands and knees." I was quite anxious. But I followed instructions. He fell to his knees behind me as I felt his hands on my hips.

Sly gave him this advice: "Apply this lube here first."

He declared, "I don't use lube." "More fun without it."

My White Knight to the rescue: "I don't give a shit. You ain't spoiling my merchandise."

There was some mumbling, but I could tell that Sly had said enough by the hush that followed. A delay ensued, during which I heard some fumbling from behind me. I couldn't bear to look.

I felt the guy's dick touch my ass at that point. I leaped. He chuckled.

"Virgin, hunh? Don't worry, you're going to love what I'm going to do to you. Now stay still and relax your sweet ass."

Staying there while he rubbed his cock between my buttocks took all my willpower. But it was at least something that I could sense that he was fully lubricated. Subsequently, I sensed his dick's head pressing on my anus. It pushed harder after that. The man restrained my forward motion by holding my hips. As the cock applied more pressure, I sensed my anus expanding. and extending. It hurt a little, and I whimpered more because I was expecting pain than because I was actually uncomfortable. Still, he grunted and pressed harder.

"Jesus, Sly, you weren't kidding. She has one tight little asshole!" More stress. I whimpered again, my body hurting. Only I seemed to care. Just as I was about to give up and scream, his cock's head suddenly popped into my rectum, causing my poor anus to contract and ease some of the stretching. Not excellent, but passable at least. What was stretching inside of me now? It felt somewhat unusual, but not really uncomfortable.

"Mmmm," the man muttered. He pushed deeper into me, saying, "Oh, that's much more like it. God, you're so warm and soft and tight in there. I love it. Now comes the really good part." Since he was well lubricated, the rest of his cock slipped in really effortlessly after the thick head was inside of me. I'll tell you what, the sensation of this massive cock going up in my rectum was strange. Not horrible, but quite unique. He continued to descend further. I felt his flat groin against my ass cheeks, and he paused. I could finally put to rest my fears of him sticking his head out of my mouth or whatever, knowing now how deep in he could go. He halted, hands firmly on my hips, his cock deep in my ass, and I heard him groan with satisfaction. I needed the break to give myself time to adjust to this new presence inside of me. His cock in me, all warm and pulsating, was starting to feel quite fantastic, I must admit. If he had simply left it there for a time, I wouldn't have objected, but of course he had other plans.

He started to slide in and out of my behind. He would retreat till reaching the crest behind his cock, at which point he would re-enter. At first, he moved slowly. It was kind of fun, for me. "Told you you'd like it, didn't I? Nothing like a good stiff cock up her ass to quiet a woman down and make her nice and docile," he remarked, apparently hearing my soft groans. Well, I didn't exactly feel "docile," but I did stay quiet. His attitude didn't sit well with me. Naturally, my body was more interested in what felt good and how to make it feel better than it was in my evaluation of his attitude. I've discovered that my body is fairly intelligent. I started rocking my hips back and forth to emphasize the strokes of his cock inside of me, stifling any words I could have said about docility.

Before long, I heard him begin to groan, and I could feel his hands getting tighter around my hips. When this was over, there would be some red scars there, but for now, it was something else to think about. I was too preoccupied worrying about what would happen to me if he cucked inside of me. I had to wait for a short while to find out. His strokes became shorter and faster, his groans turning to gasps as his cock disappeared deep inside me. As more blood filled it, I could really feel his cock getting heavier and thicker. He thrust hard into me, then froze. As the first of his sperm traveled from his testicles to my insides, my stretched and sensitive anus felt the large vein on the bottom of his cock swell. A moment later, I experienced a delightful warmth that burst from deep within my abdomen. It continued to expand and grow. He generously announced each ejaculation with a passionate groan and a gasp, but I could still feel every one of them. I also noticed that I was breathing heavily. Perhaps because I didn't like the guy, I didn't quite reach my climax, but I have to admit that I was really near. He wouldn't have needed to do much to make me lose it. Perhaps just reach under me and give my tense breasts a quick squeeze, or perhaps touch a tight nipple. Sadly, it was not to be. It never occurred to him, I believe. I didn't really like the guy, like I mentioned.

Regardless, it was very evident to everyone, myself included, that my personal needs were not his top priority at that specific moment. He kept on cumming for a long time inside of me, gasping and groaning and generally having a great time. It seems like a long time since his last. Even as more surged in, I could feel the pressure of his quickly expanding load inside of me, searching for somewhere to disperse itself in my rectum. But last, he was finished. He was breathing heavily by then, like if he had just finished a marathon or something. He fell forward over me, lifeless, and I had to brace my arms to bear his entire weight. He bit my shoulder with his chin. In any other situation, I would have told him to go away, but I was too busy feeling all the new feelings in my belly, glowing, and trying to act a little professional, so I forced myself to wait. He finally lost his anger and took his prick out of my behind. Admittedly, when his cockhead finally escaped my anus, I felt a little abandoned. Then, as some of his abundant discharge managed to seep into daylight, I felt a warm drip down my thighs.

Did he give me a compliment? Tell me how well I performed. How do you feel? He stated to Sly, "Well, that was really nice. I will say she lived up to your promises. Good work," as if Sly was the one doing the "work," completely ignoring me as he stood up and his wet dick deflated. Sly just grinned and took the comment in stride.

"Happy you enjoyed it," he added in a humble way. Remember, it's "it," not "her." "Come back any time and be sure to tell your friends. Here's my card." His note! That he'd had business cards printed up was unknown to me. I was not sure whether to be proud, humiliated, angry, or flattered. It was obvious that we would need to speak later. Not while I was dripping with semen and completely nude, either.

My 'debt' to Sly was decreasing rather quickly—at $300, $400, and sometimes even $500. Simultaneously, my self-assurance in my recently acquired skills was increasing. It turned out that was probably not the finest new development after all. Feeling confident in my acquired abilities, I thought it would be a good idea to freelance a little to expedite the payment process. Thus, I made an investment in some professional attire: a well-fitting button-front blouse, black nylons with lace elastic tops, a short black leather skirt with a small slit on the right side, and some quite painful high heels. I went out alone one evening. I chose a night at random and, about a day beforehand, called Sly to let him know that I wouldn't be available that evening. It felt a lot like calling in to your normal work and pretending to be unwell, which was a pretty bizarre sensation. Fortunately, Sly simply hung up and muttered. It seems that he had nothing planned for me that evening.

I rode in a taxi into town. Men on foot and passing cars gave me approving looks as I strolled around in search of a decent bar. I filed the incident for further consideration, but I wasn't planning on a quickie in his car when one guy even drove over and beckoned to me. I eventually located a pleasant, calm area and stopped in for a drink. The bartender took a close look at me. Without my request, he gave me a ginger ale with a hint of food coloring and grinned at me, presumably thinking I was a good business partner. I also filed that, reminding myself to give him a tip afterwards.

It's really nice to report that the bees quickly gathered around the honey. It was my decision. I held off until a very attractive man wearing a classy suit decided to take a chance. After a long conversation, he made the proposal. "Let me try to put this as delicately as possible, and hope I won't ruin a good thing, but how much?"

"It's okay," I grinned. Well. I suppose I was a little too blatant. Make a mental note to lower your standards the next time. I told him there was no harm in asking. "Rather flattering, actually. $500."

He didn't even blink, thank God. You know, quality doesn't come cheap.

He said, "Great. Give me a minute to get a room." After that, we hailed a taxi to an undisclosed, excellent hotel. He murmured in my ear and caressed my thighs on the way. I enjoyed it.

Our room was quite nice. even featured a minibar, so we raised a glass to one another and spoke for a while. I was impressed by his perseverance, even though I was finding it increasingly challenging to continue inventing a tale about myself. However, we quickly got down to business. He unzipped and undid my blouse, leaving my black lacy bra in place. He requested me to leave my high heels and stockings on, hike up my skirt, sit in a chair, and cross my legs. That was new to me, but he could call the shots as he pleased, as I already had his $500 in my tiny handbag.

"You have the sexiest legs I think I've ever seen," stated the man. Of course, why wouldn't it be? "I'd really like to cum on them, if that's okay with you."

"Well," I replied, "I would be very happy and flattered to have you do it if that's what you would like." Please let me know how I may be of assistance.

He remarked, "You're a gorgeous woman, and I really appreciate how accommodating you have been. I'll take care of the rest; all I want is that you look hot while caressing my penis with those gorgeous, long fingers. Good?"

Great. This was going to be the easiest $500 I'd ever earned. I helped him unzip his fly, and even undid his belt for him and dropped his pants. He was already hard. I stood up close to him and kissed him while I unbuttoned his shirt. I briefly touched his cock and bent down and gave it a chaste kiss. Then I hiked up my skirt to show the tops of my nylons and sat down in front of him, again crossing my legs as seductively as I could and throwing back my shoulders to raise my breasts so that they overflowed my bra a little. He moved in close alongside me, and I started stroking his cock, slowly and delicately at first, but then with growing enthusiasm as his breath quickened. He had quite a nicely shaped and sized cock, and I must admit I rather enjoyed stroking it and feeling it come to life (I seemed to be becoming quite the connoisseur of cocks). I started by gently running my open fingers up and down the length of it, then curling them over the tip and gently squeezing it. I really had no idea what I was doing, but his increasingly ragged breathing and occasional gasps made an excellent guide. I paid particular attention to the head and the area just behind it, stroking and occasionally lightly scraping it with my red fingernails. I could feel him getting harder and harder. As we progressed, I wrapped my fingers around his shaft and slid up and down him, gradually increasing the tempo and grip as his moaning directed me to do. All the while he kept looking intently at my legs, but for whatever reason didn't reach out to touch them. Finally he gasped and moaned and grabbed his cock, the better to aim it, and started to spurt onto my stockinged thighs. It was weird, but kind of sexy in its own way. I'd never really watched a man cum before, and it was fascinating.

I felt like I owed him a little more for his generous contribution to my get out of jail fund, so I used my fingers to wipe up some of his rich product from my thighs and made a show of spreading some on my breasts and then licked my fingers slowly and lovingly and smiled up at him. That he obviously liked, watching in rapt fascination. I let him keep cumming on me, helpfully stroking and caressing him until he was thoroughly done with only a drop or two oozing out of the tiny slit. By then my thighs were pretty wet with his frothy white semen; some was on the floor and some on the chair. Housekeeping was going to be thrilled.

"Stay right there," I said, and went to get a towel from the bathroom. I made a little show out of wiping his cock and then my own legs, letting him have a close look as I stretched each one out and stroked it sensually. After that, I held the wet towel to my mouth and nose and took a puff. "Do you mind if I keep the towel as a memento of a wonderful evening?"I replied in my most sly voice, and he grinned. I was doing fantastic!

He remarked, "You know, you were really quite wonderful," after putting on his clothes. To express my gratitude, I would very much like to gift you an additional hundred. Is there any way I can contact you again?Even though he was very nice, I didn't dare give him my actual contact information because that would be asking for trouble. For a crazy moment, I wished I had one of Sly's "business cards" because I could just picture me giving it to him and telling him to call my agent. Jeez. So, I made up a phone number, just a few random digits off my real one so it would look authentic (if it turned out to be a real number it would make for an interesting call). I added my current name, pocketed the extra $100, kissed him tenderly, and then I left, hiding in the lobby until I was certain he wasn't following me, and I took a taxi home because, well, I could afford it. I also bought new stockings.

Once a few days had passed and I had still not heard from Sly, I decided to give him a call myself. When he picked up, I could tell I had interrupted him mid-thought, so I was succinct. "Look, I've been doing pretty good by you," I said, "and maybe I can ask for a favor." There was silence on the other end. "Don't sweat, "I just asked that next time you get me a regular fuck." Just good ol' fashioned man-on-woman fuck, no anal or oral. Is that something you can do?"

A lengthy moment passed. "Are we becoming a little picky?"Honey, you don't call the shots here," he remarked with a laugh. You must realize that. However, I must say that up until now, you've been surprisingly good for a princess. Maybe you should take a break, I suppose. Let me see if I can help. Come by on Thursday at regular hour. But no guarantees. It all depends on what I can find. However, don't expect five hundred dollars. Generally speaking, guys only spend more on things they can't buy at home."

When I arrived at Sly's apartment on Thursday, I gave him the fresh $500 right away. After accepting it, his eyes furrowed and he said, "You been free-lancing, haven't you?"

"All right? You say what about that? Why does it matter to you what I do with my leisure time as long as you receive your money?"

He said, "I got an interest in you, so that's why I care. Free lancin' is dangerous stuff." You are ignorant about this industry. You might have suffered harm. I want no harm done to you. I can keep you safe because I am familiar with the system. With me, there won't be any bad shocks."

"I acknowledge your care, but whether you like it or not, I'm not your property. We're done when the money I owe you is paid. Story ends here. For the rest of my life, stay away."

He was obviously offended by that, but really, what could he do?

Finally, he answered, "Okay, okay. Just be careful, would ya? I like that. It sounds so very professional. "Well, I got a client for you for tonight," he says, calling me a "client." With a strange smile on his face, I can't help but notice that he said that. Still, being the good girl that I am, I went to the bedroom, where I always changed behind closed doors. I know it sounds strange considering my responsibilities and my relationship with Sly, but I felt that it was necessary to maintain a degree of reserve that I would lose if I barked around naked in front of him.

Entering the bedroom, I undressed and reached into the drawer where Sly usually kept my working negligee. Then, in complete disregard for what I had just said, I rushed out into the living room, completely nude, and held Sly's package out in front of me.

"You've got to be kidding me! I'm not going to wear this clothes! Goddamn, I'm a lawyer! What on earth is the purpose of this?"At that point, I hurled the Dallas Cowboys cheerleader's outfit at him and exuded fury and indignation while standing with my hands on my naked hips.

And the son of a bitch just continued to smile, broader still.

"Slow down. You explicitly requested a straight-up fuck, if you recall. Alright, here's one for you. All he wants to do is fuck a Dallas cheerleader, that's all. Look, dressing up for once and fulfilling the guy's dream won't kill you. I'm betting there's a bonus in it for us if you succeed. You can do it, I promise. Put it down. In addition, he will arrive in a few minutes, so what can I say if you refuse to do it?"

I gave him a scowl and yelled, "Fuck it," in an effort to keep my dignity. Alright. But will you please warn me the next time?"and proceeded to put on the costume by going back to the bedroom. Before I shut the door, I could feel his avaricious gaze pursuing my nude posterior.

A few minutes later, all dolled up, I strolled out; Sly was

getting the hang of this; the boots were a little loose, the halter a little tight, but generally it fit quite well. When I walked out, he just stared.

"Jesus, you look good in that outfit," he replied. "Our boy's gonna cum in his pants if you aren't careful."

When the doorbell rang, it was showtime. I had just about settled into a decorous pose on the couch, considering my tight short shorts.

The man was middle-aged, not particularly attractive, just average. As soon as he entered, he looked around and noticed me sitting there. I must admit, I liked the look of surprise on his face. However, Sly quickly shifted his focus to business matters, and I watched as money was exchanged. I guess I had passed muster.

I have to admit that I was pleased by the grin on his face, like a child with a new toy on Christmas morning. I was actually starting to like this. Sly took the guy over to the couch, and I got up as elegantly as I could in this clothing.

"You are so incredibly beautiful," stated the man. "What's your name?"

Saying "thank you," I spoke. "Tiffany." That seemed like something you might call a cheerleader, what the hell? "You're being kind when you say that. You don't look too bad yourself."

"I've watched you girls perform since I was a teenager," he continued. As long as they show you, I don't care which team prevails. I've even followed you on social media and owned your calendars. You are much more stunning in person than I could have ever imagined."

He was so into this, wow. I couldn't tell if he was just getting himself up into his own little fantasy or if he really thought I was real. Anyway, I thought I should go along with it. Saying "thank you," I spoke. "Thank you very much for that. To show my gratitude, I would be honored to perform any task you ask of me in order to make you feel good." Was I overt or something?

He answered, "I'd very much like that." Come on over here, please. If it is okay with you, I would like to kiss you."

I moved a few paces in his direction. I tried my hardest to walk sensually even though it was difficult in these boots. In any case, my client seemed grateful (I love the word: so professional). I was only centimeters away from his face. His hands found my naked waist as he reached out. I sensed the repressed energy within them. I believe that he was hesitant to touch me because he thought it would shatter the illusion that I wasn't real. I raised my face to him in an appealing manner, and he tentatively leaned over to plant a kiss on me. I enthusiastically kissed him back after raising my arms and taking his face in my hands. I was really starting to warm to this poor guy. He showed such deference.

I pushed my tongue between his lips and pressed my hips into his. I undid his shirt button, raised his undergarment, undid the small knot that secured my halter, and gently placed my exposed breasts on his flesh. His breath stopped and then started to come in faster. As he struggled to fasten the belt and buttons on my tight little white shorts, I moved his hands down to the belt and inserted my tongue deeper into his lips.

I led his hands to my shorts' waistband and pushed him to slide them down over my hips while I continued to kiss him and press my breasts against him so he could feel my nipples. I slightly retreated and let him to ease them down to my boots. He bowed to pass his face over my abdomen and chest. Naturally, I had nothing on underneath the shorts when I felt his nose brush my pussy. With his assistance, I managed to remove the shorts and reveal the boots and open halter that beautifully accentuated my breasts.

I took his hand and steered him toward the couch. In my hands, the poor guy was like putty. Clearly, he didn't mind if I took the initiative. It felt rather empowering. I gave him another kiss and reclined in the couch. I crossed my legs politely for a while. There's no need in disclosing anything ahead of schedule! I waited for him to get close to me before taking off and sliding down his pants. I played with the wet area of pre-cum on his shorts and caressed the bulge.

By then, he was breathing quite heavily, and I didn't want Sly's prophecy to come true, so I politely leaned back to allow him a better look and a moment to collect his breath. I made sure my long hair was attractively spread out on the cushion behind my head and my breasts were fully exposed as I laid out on the couch. I then pretended to spread my legs just enough to be visibly inviting and gave him the most seductive smile I could manage. That certainly put an end to his hesitation. His prick made a sudden movement. In one swift motion, he removed the remaining portion of his shirt and undershirt, then settled between my knees on the couch.

"You have no idea of how long I've dreamed of just this moment," he replied.

I replied, "Then don't rush." "We've got plenty of time, and I want you to enjoy every minute." That wasn't really true, though, because later that evening I had some office work to do for my day job. However, that job's income was nothing like as good as this one's.

I extended my arms and pulled him up onto me. His penis slid right into me. He sighed. After kissing him and pulling his head down, I put my hands on his buttocks and urged him to start fucking me. He moved in and out, a little cautiously at first, but with time, confidence and vigor growing as I sighed and groaned in silent. It did feel quite wonderful, though. He raised his arms to support his chest so he could see my breasts move while his hips plunged harder and deeper into me with each stroke as our lubrication increased. I was becoming quite invested in this! My skin started to quiver and I started to feel hot. The next thing I knew, I was coming, gasping and trembling, and all hell broke free. No need to pretend!

That satisfied him. With a final powerful push, his cock burst inside of me. I was acutely aware of the waves of hot cum that were surging into my very responsive vagina and could feel it throbbing. over and over. He moaned and jerked and, oddly enough, shed a tear or two. In my opinion, he did. It was difficult to tell with all of our combined gasping, writhing, and moaning. When your life's goal is finally accomplished, you could feel some remorse.

He continued to bump into me. His discharge ran down between my legs and I felt it come back up. His warm come flew into me as his cock pumped four, five, and six times. You truly can have too much of a good thing, even though it felt amazing. His ejaculations ceased abruptly, but it transpired that he was only hesitating, as he proceeded to ejaculate five or six times in quick succession before I could reply. Whoa. I understood that he was accomplishing a long-held ambition, but really, had he been hoarding his love potion up until now?

But eventually, his cock stopped pulsing inside of me, and his arms failed, causing his body to collapse upon me, squeezing my breasts and breathing heavily with his head tucked in my neck.

"Oh my God," he uttered. "That was everything I'd ever dreamed of, only better." I felt quite good about myself, didn't I? I am a sainthood candidate. Tiffany Saint. having a cunt.

I let him to lie down on me and gave him gentle back rubs while he healed. Despite my want to nip on his ear, I refrained from doing so since I thought it would trigger another outburst and keep us there till the next day. After all, I did have things to do. He finally let out a long moan and removed his significantly smaller cock from me. He rose from the couch, smiling at me the entire time and not missing an opportunity to admire my artistically arranged nude body, shimmering with sweat from our efforts, and the not-so-small pool of sperm between my legs. He turned to face Sly, who had been silently seated the entire time.

"It is truly amazing how much you have made this possible," he remarked. "She fulfilled all of your promises and then some. All I can hope is that you understand how fortunate you are to have her." If he didn't, I certainly did.

"Yeah, well, okay," Sly said as he exited. Always kind.

The man added, "Please, take this," pulling a sizable bill out of his wallet and giving it to Sly. "Tonight was worth every penny of it." And with that, he was off, a very happy customer.

I got off the couch as soon as the door shut. Retying the halter, I dried off, put on the shorts, and faced Sly. "All right, let it out. What was the small package he gave you at the conclusion?"

Looking wonderfully innocent, Sly continued, "Just a little thank-you note." "I'll credit your account with your half after I find out how we made out tonight. Look, I've got exactly what you wanted—a straightforward, traditional fuck. Give me a little praise."

I answered, "Um, no." "That small 'thank-you note' sounds like something I'd like to see for myself. Except for the fact that you're a bastard, you've been rather honest with me, therefore I've accepted our arrangement thus far. Don't mess things up right now.

Sly withdrew a $1,000 cash reluctantly from his pocket.

"Jesus Christ," I declared. "And just how much of that were you planning to share?"

"Now, simple, easy, honey. Let's avoid getting our underwear tangled." Well, I wasn't sure how to take that because I wasn't wearing any underwear at the time. That wasn't the point, though.

"I want at the very least half of that credited to my debt," I said. "I worked harder than usual tonight. I was the one who gave that poor guy the ride of his life by dressing up like that stupid costume. You charged that to my phone. And now we are really totally even, by my accounting. I take the pictures and everything else you have, and I regain control over my life."

That's when my life turned into a divergence. And the reason I'm writing all of this down is so that I can comprehend what transpired at the time.

Sly remained silent for what felt like an eternity. He finally asked me to take a seat. Sitting there in my rather rumpled Dallas cheerleader costume, I felt like I knew exactly what was going to happen, and I felt like a complete outsider, but I dared not break the moment's momentum.

Okay, he replied. "You're a bright young lady, so I won't try to make light of you. It's undeniable that you fulfilled my request for the pictures. Just and equitable, without grumbling. Along with anything else I have on you, they are yours."

I grinned from ear to ear and began to stand. He answered, "But first, hear me out." "All right, I did use you. I didn't injure you, though, did I? Was there ever anything I put you in that you couldn't handle? You've truly enjoyed working with me, admit it. Even though I'm not a saint, you can trust that I will defend you because, well, you're really good at what you do, and I value that greatly. I believe you've realized how talented you truly are, and you enjoy it. You seem to enjoy the work, too. Additionally, I believe you're intelligent enough to understand that trying something on your own puts you at risk of injury. Now that you're free, you have two options: stay with me or give it all up and squander your skill on a regular nine to five job. While you do what you love and are extremely excellent at, I keep you secure and stocked with wonderful, well-paying clients so that we can both make a ton of money. Alternatively, you may simply return to your regular work and act as if the excitement and money you've earned over the past several weeks haven't happened."

Whoa. That was a direct quote. I was shocked beyond belief. These past few weeks, all I could think about was paying Sly back and returning to my life as I knew it. Was it all I actually wanted, though, now that it was a reality? As God would have it, I had changed as a woman in just one month. Sly called me "Princess". What was it that I was expecting? Living in Greenwich, marrying a lawyer, going to cocktail parties at tennis clubs, volunteering at the Women's Auxiliary Fill-in-the-Blank? I had discovered a wild and dark side to myself during the past few weeks, and I kind of enjoyed it. Furthermore, I excelled at what I did.

And Sly, too? Let me tell you, girls will never see Sly as their ideal prince charming. But as long as I deliver for him, I know I can rely on him to stand by me. Yes, that is just selfishness. Nevertheless, having someone watch out for you can be kind of nice, and there are worse foundations for a relationship than complete honesty.

I believe it's pretty evident which way this is going to go after reading what I wrote again. I wish for [my fiancé] to find a lifelong partner. Well, not me. Perhaps one day I'll even wed a man who will be incredibly surprised by me. Yes, I realize that in a few more years I'll outgrow this new double life, but in the meanwhile, I'm not quitting my day job, which even seems to have a future. They notice talent when they see it, albeit a different kind of talent than I've been discussing. Nevertheless, I'm aware that occasionally, while working on a tedious legal brief at my desk, I'll just lose myself in the momentary recollections of a memorable night out with a wonderful client, leaving my coworkers perplexed as to why I have a mysterious Mona Lisa smile on my face. Hehe. Lisa Mondavi. mysterious smile. You don't think she would... Nope.

And so it is. I sincerely hope that my short rant is never seen, but since you are reading it, it must have gotten out somehow. My fault. I can't help but not burn it, even though I should. I may require it at some point to reconsider my choice. But please, help me. Please, please, keep my secret to yourself if you happen to run into me at a bar one night while I'm dressed in my (other) business attire and you want to try some of my offerings.

Acknowledgments

The Glory of this book's success goes to God Almighty and my beautiful Family, Fans, Readers & well-wishers, Customers, and Friends for their endless support and encouragement.

About The Author

I've spent nearly a decade penning romantic novels. As a passionate writer of erotica, I craft dark, romantic erotica. Anime Naked Truth Se of Sacred Sexuality: Forbidden Seducing Short Stories of an Erotica Nude Sexy Girl Poster. Alongside Erotic Mystery Fiction, Victorian Erotica Sex, Black & African American Erotica, Euthanasia, Daddy Teaching, Forced Domination, Alpha Monster Cuckold, and BDSM for Adults, there's an Erotic Fiction in Kinky Family. I write dark, sensual romance because I adore the power of darkness and everything that it entails. Romance novels have always been my favorite kind of books, and now I'm writing them. The idea that you will like reading and enjoying my fiction as much as I enjoy pushing the frontiers of sexual pleasure in my writing thrills me more than anything else.